PAUL ROBESON

PAUL ROBESON

Eloise Greenfield

illustrated by George Ford

LEE & LOW BOOKS Inc.
New York

This edition of *Paul Robeson* reflects information that had not been published at the time of the original edition.

AUTHOR'S SOURCES

Adams, Russell L. *Great Negroes Past and Present*, 3rd ed. Chicago: Afro-Am Publishing, 1969.

Foner, Philip S., ed. *Paul Robeson Speaks: Writings, Speeches, Interviews, 1918–1974*. New York: Brunner-Mazel Publishers, 1978.

Gilliam, Dorothy. "Tribute to a Baaad Dude, a Living Hero." *Washington Post*, sec. B, April 16, 1973.

Graham, Shirley. *Paul Robeson: Citizen of the World*. New York: Julian Messner, 1971.

Paul Robeson Archives. *Salute to Paul Robeson: A Cultural Celebration of His 75th Birthday*. New York: Paul Robeson Archives, 1973.

Robeson, Eslanda Goode. *Paul Robeson, Negro*. New York: Harper & Brothers, 1930.

Robeson, Paul. *Here I Stand*. Boston: Beacon Press, 1958.

Robeson, Paul, Jr. "Paul Robeson: Black Warrior." *Freedomways* 11, no. 1. New York: Freedomways Associates, 1971.

———. *The Undiscovered Paul Robeson: An Artist's Journey, 1898–1939*. New York: John Wiley & Sons, 2001.

Robeson, Susan. *The Whole World in His Hands: A Pictorial Biography of Paul Robeson*. Secaucus, NJ: Citadel Press, 1981.

Rollins, Charlemae. *Famous Negro Entertainers of Stage, Screen and TV*. New York: Dodd, Mead, 1967.

Seton, Marie. *Paul Robeson*. London: Dennis Dobson, 1958.

QUOTATION SOURCES

p. 37: "I must . . . dying." Seton, Marie. *Paul Robeson*, p. 112.

p. 38: "The glory . . . father." Robeson, Paul. *Here I Stand*, p. 6.
  "Thank . . . last," "Thank . . . *moving!*" Ibid., p. 119.

p. 40: "Though . . . retirement," "you . . . dying.'" Robeson, Susan. *The Whole World in His Hands: A Pictorial Biography of Paul Robeson*, p. 244.

Text copyright © 2009, 1975 by Eloise Greenfield
Illustrations copyright © 1975 by George Ford
All rights reserved. No part of this book may be reproduced, transmitted, or stored in an information retrieval system in any form or by any means, electronic, mechanical, photocopying, recording, or otherwise, without written permission from the publisher.
LEE & LOW BOOKS Inc., 95 Madison Avenue, New York, NY 10016   leeandlow.com

Manufactured in China
Book design by Tania Garcia
Book production by The Kids at Our House

The text is set in 13.5 Della Robbia
The illustrations are rendered in acrylic on illustration board

(HC) 10 9 8 7 6 5 4 3 2 1
(PB) 10 9 8 7 6 5 4 3 2 1
First LEE & LOW Edition, 2009

Library of Congress Cataloging-in-Publication Data

Greenfield, Eloise.
Paul Robeson / Eloise Greenfield ; illustrated by George Ford.
   p. cm.
   Summary: "A biography of Paul Robeson, who overcame racial discrimination to become a world-famous African American athlete, actor, singer, and civil rights activist"—Provided by publisher.
   ISBN 978-1-60060-256-6 (hardcover) —
   ISBN 978-1-60060-262-7 (pbk.)
1. Robeson, Paul, 1898-1976—Juvenile literature. 2. African Americans—Biography—Juvenile literature. 3. Actors—United States—Biography—Juvenile literature. 4. Singers—United States—Biography—Juvenile literature. 5. Political activists—United States—Biography—Juvenile literature. I. Ford, George, ill. II. Title.
E185.97.R63G74 2009
782.0092—dc22
[B]   2008030420

The name Paul Robeson brings back wonderful memories from my childhood in the 1930s and 1940s. I remember hearing him sing. I heard him on the radio, not on television, because there was no television then. I loved his voice. It was low, very low, and had just the right amount of trembling, not too much and not too little. He sang as if he really meant the words of the songs.

Paul Robeson was very famous, and many people loved him. They loved his singing and acting, and they admired him for the things he said in his speeches. His admirers were not happy when, in the late 1940s, some people made trouble for him and kept him from performing. That trouble is a part of the story this book will tell. It will also tell of Paul Robeson's courage and his desire to help people all over the world.

A large part of this story is about the boy, Paul, and his growing-up years. Family was important to him and helped him to develop his talents. Family, friends, and neighbors also helped him to recover from a great loss he suffered when he was very young.

Paul Robeson grew up to be a man the world will never forget. I hope you enjoy meeting him.

Eloise Greenfield, 2009

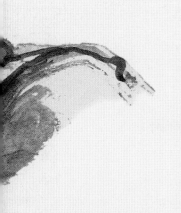

When William D. Robeson was a boy, he was enslaved. He was not free, and he was forced to work without pay on a plantation in North Carolina. He hated being enslaved. He hated it so much that when he was fifteen years old, he did a very dangerous thing.

He ran away.

If he had been caught, the enslaver would have beaten him with a whip or killed him. But William Robeson was determined to be free.

He escaped to the North, where he went to school. After he graduated from college, he married Maria Louisa Bustill and became pastor of the Witherspoon Street Presbyterian Church in Princeton, New Jersey.

Princeton was a small town built around a big university. The university was for white students. White people who lived in the town often went to meetings and parties at the university. Black people went to meetings and parties at Reverend Robeson's church.

On April 9, 1898, in the parsonage of the church, the youngest child of Reverend and Mrs. Robeson was born. They named him Paul Leroy Robeson.

Reverend Robeson was fifty-three years old, not a young man, when Paul was born. Mrs. Robeson was sickly and almost blind. Even with her thick glasses, she could not see very well. Still, Paul's mother, father, sister, and three brothers were all very happy to welcome the new baby into the family.

When Paul was almost three years old, his father lost his position at the church because of an argument among the members. This was a hard blow for Reverend Robeson. Yet, in his quiet, strong way, he went about finding a new way to support his family. He bought a horse named Bess and a wagon, and people who lived in Princeton paid him to take away the ashes from their coal furnaces.

Paul often watched Bess pull the wagon into the backyard so that his father could dump the ashes. Paul and Bess became good friends.

Sometimes Reverend Robeson or Paul's brother Reeve hitched Bess to a large carriage and drove passengers where they wanted to go. Some of the passengers were students from Princeton University. More than once, Reeve fought these students for making insulting remarks about black people.

Paul admired Reeve, Bill, Marian, and Ben, and they loved their little brother. Reeve taught Paul always to stand up for his rights. Paul was big for his age, and his brothers taught him to play football. Sometimes in the evenings after dinner, the children sang. Paul was happiest when Bill was home on vacation from college and the whole family could be together.

But when Paul was six years old, a tragic accident upset the family's happiness. One day when his mother was cleaning the house, she bumped into the coal stove that kept the house warm. A hot coal fell on her long dress, setting it on fire, and she was burned to death.

At first Paul could not believe that his mother was really dead. Later he knew it was true because he missed her so much. Relatives and friends who lived nearby invited the younger Robeson children to their homes for dinner, or to spend days at a time. Like the Robesons, these families didn't have much money, but they were glad to share their homes. They were full of love for the children and tried to make them feel better.

Paul grew very close to his father. They played checkers together and read together. His father taught him to recite poetry and speeches, and helped him study his homework.

Paul liked school. Once in a while a teacher had to punish him for not behaving, but he always did his work. He had learned from his father the importance of doing his best. Paul also learned other things by watching and listening to his father. He learned to love words—written words and spoken words. He learned to be proud of being black. He learned that people should do the things they really believe in.

A few years after Mrs. Robeson's death, Reverend Robeson again

became pastor of a church. The church was in Westfield, near Princeton. Later he had a church in Somerville, also near Princeton.

Paul was proud when he sat in church and listened to his father's sermons. He could see that the words meant a lot to the members of the church. They liked what Reverend Robeson was saying, and they liked the rhythm of his deep bass voice.

Paul sang in the church choir. He loved music, especially the black music called spirituals. Spirituals are religious songs. They are a mixture of the music black people had known in Africa and the music and words they added after they were kidnapped to America.

At Somerville High School, Paul sang the solos in the glee club. He liked to sing, and he sang well, but he didn't think he would want to be a singer when he grew up. He *knew* he didn't want to be an actor. One year his school had given a performance of *Othello,* a play written more than four hundred years ago by William Shakespeare. Paul played the part of an African general. It was the main part, and Paul was so nervous that he promised himself he would never try acting again.

Years later Paul would be famous all over the world for his great acting in *Othello* and other plays, and for his singing. But he did not know that then.

Summers Paul went to Rhode Island with Ben. He worked in the kitchen of a hotel for rich people, and Ben worked as a waiter.

At school, Paul played football, baseball, and basketball. He was on the track team. He made speeches as a member of the debating club. Still he found time for study, and in 1915 Paul graduated with

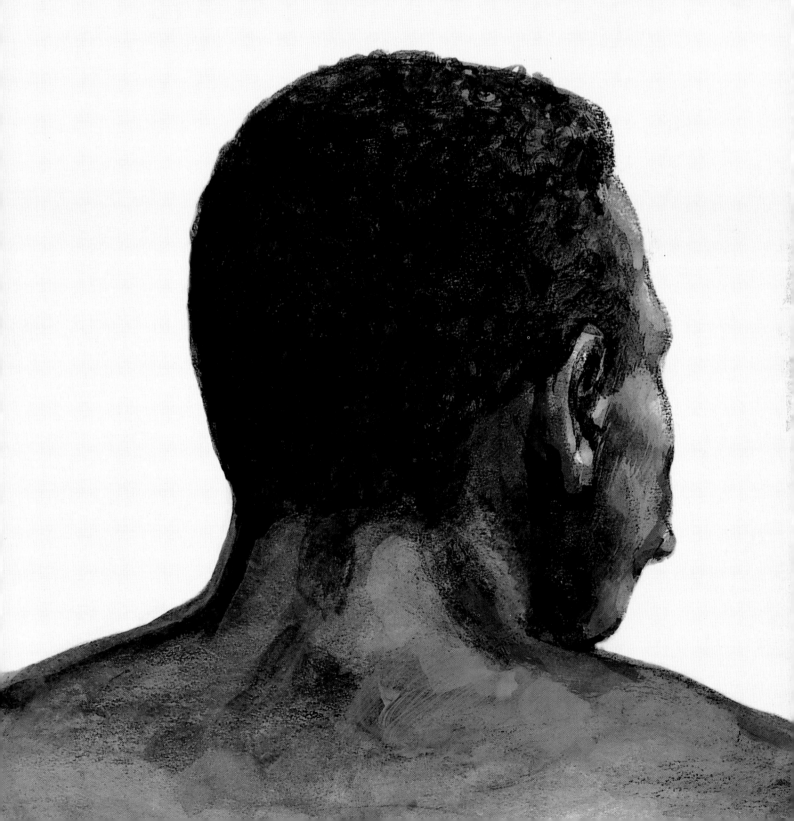

honors. He won a four-year scholarship to Rutgers College, which later became Rutgers University, and would not have to pay to go to college.

Paul was very tall now, big boned and broad shouldered. He was a dark, proud, and rather quiet young man looking forward to college.

At Rutgers, there was only one other black student. There had been only a few black students at Paul's high school, and he had had problems with some of the white students and teachers. There were problems at Rutgers, too.

Although Paul was allowed to sing in the glee club, he could not attend the parties that were held after the musical programs or travel to other towns with the glee club. When he tried out for football, the other players did not want a black player on the team. On the first day of practice, the other players kept piling up on Paul and beating him with their fists.

Paul went home with a sprained shoulder and bruises on his face and body. While he was healing, he had time to think about whether or not he wanted to try out again. He hated being hurt, but he didn't want to be a quitter.

Paul also knew that if he made the team, it would give hope to other young black athletes. He went back to practice determined to make it. He knew that he was big and strong and that he had been the star player on his high school team. If the other boys played fair, he could show the coach what he could do.

On the first play, Paul made a tackle, pulling the boy carrying the ball down with him. Another player ran over, lifted his foot, and stamped on Paul's hand. Pain from the cleats on the bottom of the player's football shoe shot through Paul's fingers.

Paul was mad. The pain and the unfairness made him as mad as he had ever been. On the next play, he picked up the player who had attacked him and lifted him up over his head. Just as Paul started to slam the boy to the ground, the coach ran up to him.

"Paul, you're on the team!" the coach yelled. "I'm picking you for the team!"

Paul put the boy down.

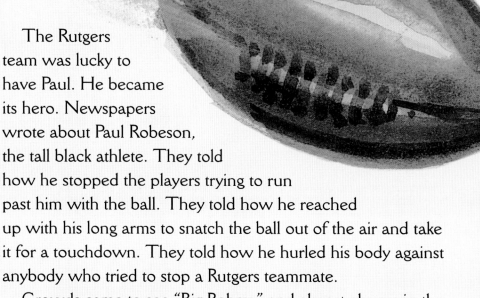

The Rutgers team was lucky to have Paul. He became its hero. Newspapers wrote about Paul Robeson, the tall black athlete. They told how he stopped the players trying to run past him with the ball. They told how he reached up with his long arms to snatch the ball out of the air and take it for a touchdown. They told how he hurled his body against anybody who tried to stop a Rutgers teammate.

Crowds came to see "Big Robey," and almost always in the crowd was Reverend Robeson, proudly watching his son.

Paul and his father were still close. Whenever Paul went home for a weekend, they spent hours together. Paul had decided to be a lawyer, and his father was disappointed. He wanted Paul to be a minister. Reverend Robeson realized, though, that his son was growing up and had to make his own decisions.

Reverend Robeson died near the end of Paul's third year of college. Paul was sad when he returned to Rutgers for his last year. His father would not be in the audience when he graduated.

Graduation day came in 1919 when Paul was twenty-one years old. He had won many honors in college. He had been elected to Phi Beta Kappa, a group of outstanding students. He had been a debating champion. He had won awards in four sports. Twice, he had been named All-American End, which meant that Paul was one of the best college football players in the United States.

As the student with the best grades in the whole graduating class, Paul was chosen to make the farewell speech. From the stage, he said good-bye to Rutgers for himself and his classmates.

The following year Paul moved to New York City to attend Columbia University Law School. Weekends he played professional football to earn money. Most of his free time was spent in Harlem, where he lived. Harlem was the part of New York City where many black people lived and worked. Paul saw plays at the Lafayette Theater. He visited friends and went to parties.

At the parties everyone loved to hear him sing. A friend would play the piano, and Paul would sing spirituals. He sang about enslaved people being a long way from home and about enslaved children leaving slavery, riding the train to freedom. The room would grow very quiet as people listened to Paul's deep, throbbing voice.

Paul's speaking voice was as rich and deep toned as his singing voice. When the Harlem Young Men's Christian Association (YMCA) decided to give a play, Paul's friends asked him to take a part in it. Paul played the main part, and this time he wasn't as nervous as he had been in high school. People told him that he was a good actor. He didn't take them seriously. He was going to be a lawyer.

Then something wonderful happened to Paul. A friend introduced him to Eslanda Goode, who was a chemist at a hospital in New York. Her friends called her Essie. Paul and Essie fell in love, and in August 1921, they were married.

The next summer Paul was invited to England. A theater company needed a black actor, and someone who had seen Paul act suggested him for the job.

Paul went alone to England this first time. On other visits, he and Essie went together and enjoyed traveling to the different towns and cities. It was in England that Paul met Lawrence Brown, who became a good friend.

Lawrence Brown was a pianist. He loved spirituals as much
as Paul did and not only played them on the piano but arranged
them. He put the notes in order and wrote them on music paper.

When Paul graduated from law school in 1923, it was hard for a black lawyer, especially a new one, to find work. Paul finally got a job with a white law firm, where some members of the firm refused to work with him. After a few weeks, he left.

Now Paul was out of a job, but producers were asking him to be in their plays. They wanted to pay Paul Robeson for his talent. More and more, he appeared on the stage. In some of the plays, he both acted and sang.

Paul had never taken acting or singing lessons. He acted by making himself feel the way he thought the character would feel. He spent hours reading his part over and over. Sometimes he sat in a quiet place and thought about it.

Paul also appeared on musical programs called concerts. Lawrence Brown came to New York, and in 1925, he and Paul gave a concert of all-black music. A concert with one person singing spirituals and other black songs was a new idea. Many people wanted to hear this music. They filled all the seats in the theater, and some people even had to stand.

Lawrence Brown played the piano and Paul sang. Paul made his voice sometimes loud, sometimes soft, sometimes happy, sometimes sad. Some notes he chopped off and some he held a long, long time. Every note had to be just right. He wanted the audience to feel what he felt about black music.

At the end of the concert, the audience cheered and yelled for more. They did not want the concert to end.

Paul Robeson and Lawrence Brown became a famous team. For years they traveled all over the United States and to other parts of the world to give concerts. They went to Africa, France, the West Indies, Russia, England, and other places. Paul also made recordings and performed in plays and movies and on the radio.

Paul was in England when his son was born in New York on November 2, 1927. Paul and Essie named the baby Paul, Jr. Sometimes the baby traveled with them.

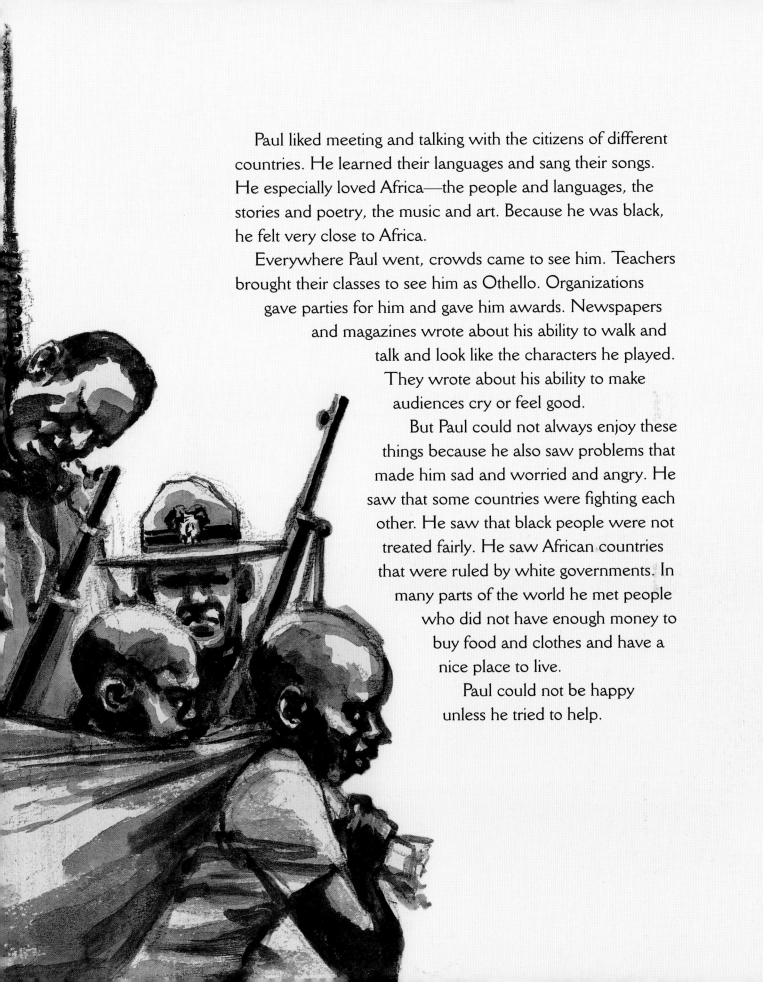

Paul liked meeting and talking with the citizens of different countries. He learned their languages and sang their songs. He especially loved Africa—the people and languages, the stories and poetry, the music and art. Because he was black, he felt very close to Africa.

Everywhere Paul went, crowds came to see him. Teachers brought their classes to see him as Othello. Organizations gave parties for him and gave him awards. Newspapers and magazines wrote about his ability to walk and talk and look like the characters he played. They wrote about his ability to make audiences cry or feel good.

But Paul could not always enjoy these things because he also saw problems that made him sad and worried and angry. He saw that some countries were fighting each other. He saw that black people were not treated fairly. He saw African countries that were ruled by white governments. In many parts of the world he met people who did not have enough money to buy food and clothes and have a nice place to live.

Paul could not be happy unless he tried to help.

Paul began to make speeches at his concerts. After he sang, he talked. He talked about black freedom, good jobs for everyone, and peace. Audiences listened. Many people wanted to hear what Paul had to say.

But not everybody.

Not everybody wanted Paul to talk about problems, but he had to do what he believed was right. He often thought of his father. Paul wanted to be as strong as his father had been.

As the years passed, Paul continued to speak out, and he worked, too. He marched with signs in front of theaters where black people had to sit in the back or in the balcony. He marched in front of the offices of baseball teams that would not hire black ballplayers. He went to see the president of the United States to protest the killings of black people in the South. He started a newspaper called *Freedom*. He helped to start groups that worked for black freedom. He wrote articles for magazines.

Often Paul went to large peace meetings held by communists. Communists believe in a different kind of government than the one in the United States. Many Americans did not like communists and were afraid they would make the United States a communist country.

In the 1940s and 1950s, some members of Congress in Washington, D.C., where laws are made, began to punish communists and their friends. The communists lost their jobs or had to go to jail. The people who wanted Paul Robeson to stop talking about problems began to punish him for having communist friends.

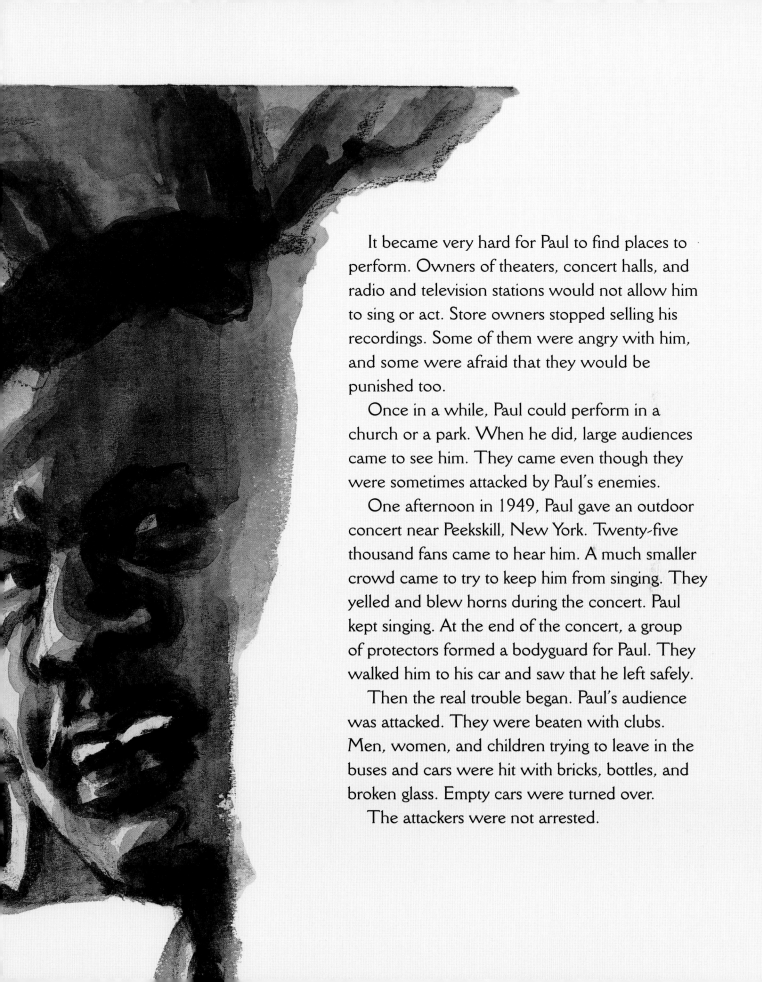

It became very hard for Paul to find places to perform. Owners of theaters, concert halls, and radio and television stations would not allow him to sing or act. Store owners stopped selling his recordings. Some of them were angry with him, and some were afraid that they would be punished too.

Once in a while, Paul could perform in a church or a park. When he did, large audiences came to see him. They came even though they were sometimes attacked by Paul's enemies.

One afternoon in 1949, Paul gave an outdoor concert near Peekskill, New York. Twenty-five thousand fans came to hear him. A much smaller crowd came to try to keep him from singing. They yelled and blew horns during the concert. Paul kept singing. At the end of the concert, a group of protectors formed a bodyguard for Paul. They walked him to his car and saw that he left safely.

Then the real trouble began. Paul's audience was attacked. They were beaten with clubs. Men, women, and children trying to leave in the buses and cars were hit with bricks, bottles, and broken glass. Empty cars were turned over.

The attackers were not arrested.

The next year, Paul was told by the government that he could not visit other countries.

"Stop talking and just sing," he was told.

Paul said, "No." He said he had the right both to travel and speak. He took his case to court for judges to decide.

While the judges were considering his case, Paul could not leave the United States. But his voice could.

Several times he sang at the line between the United States and Canada. He stood on a stage in the United States, on one side of the line. His audience sat in a park in Canada, on the other side of the line.

Once, almost a thousand people went to a concert in England, and although Paul was not there, his voice traveled across the Atlantic Ocean by telephone. The last song he sang was "Old Man River." One line in this song says that a man is tired of living and scared of dying. Paul changed this line. He sang, "I must keep fighting until I'm dying."

Paul Robeson kept fighting. He kept fighting for freedom for all human beings, and he kept fighting for himself. He had to go to court many times to get back his right to travel. Finally, in 1958, after eight years of trying, he won. He could travel again.

In the years that followed, millions of black people in America began to feel close to their African heritage. They marched for their rights and for better jobs. Some black singers and actors spoke out for black freedom, as Paul Robeson had.

In 1959, Paul began to have health problems. He was not always well enough to travel and perform. Eventually he had to retire. He and Essie lived in England, Russia, and Germany before returning to their home in New York. In 1965, Essie died after a long illness.

Paul Robeson wrote a book called *Here I Stand*. It is about his life as a boy and his beliefs as a man. In this book he said, "The glory of my boyhood years was my father."

Like his father, Paul Robeson was determined to be free. He said that although black people could not yet sing "Thank God Almighty, we're free at last," they could sing "Thank God Almighty, we're *moving*!"

Paul Robeson died on January 23, 1976.

Afterword

In April 1973, almost three years before the death of Paul Robeson, a seventy-fifth birthday celebration was held for him at Carnegie Hall in New York City. Twenty famous stars performed in front of a large audience. Paul was too sick to attend. His son went in his place. Paul, Jr., was as close to his father as Paul Robeson had been to his.

Since Paul Robeson's death, much has been written about him—plays and films that dramatize his life, newspaper and magazine articles, and books. Countless honors have been given in memory of his contributions. In 1995, more than seventy-five years after Paul was the Rutgers football hero, he was made a member of the College Football Hall of Fame. In February 1998, he was named the winner of a Grammy Lifetime Achievement Award for his music. And throughout that year, people across the United States and the world celebrated Paul Robeson's one hundredth birthday. In 2004, the United States Postal Service issued, as part of its Black Heritage series, a first-class Paul Robeson postage stamp.

During his illness, Paul Robeson spoke of his feelings about his work. "Though ill health has compelled my retirement," he said, "you can be sure that in my heart I go on singing, 'I must keep fighting until I'm dying.'"

Paul Robeson lived and sang a purposeful life. The people of the world are fortunate that, because of recordings, we can still hear the power, the richness, and the beauty of his voice.

E. G.